MONSTER BUG

by Linda Hayward
illustrated by Diane Palmisciano

The Kane Press
New York

Acknowledgements: Our thanks to Marc Feldman, PhD (Physics, UC Berkeley), Professor, University of Rochester and Dr. Richard Moyer, Professor of Science Education, University of Michigan—Dearborn, for helping us make this book as accurate as possible.

Book Design/Art Direction: Edward Miller

Library of Congress Cataloging-in-Publication Data

Hayward, Linda.
  Monster bug / by Linda Hayward ; illustrated by Diane
Palmisciano.
      p. cm. — (Science solves it!)
Summary: After cousins Kyle and Jenna discover how their older siblings managed to scare them by using shadows, they use the same trick to get revenge.
  ISBN 1-57565-135-1 (pbk. : alk. paper)
  [1. Teasing—Fiction. 2. Cousins—Fiction. 3. Brothers and sisters—Fiction.] I. Palmisciano, Diane, ill. II. Title. III. Series.
  PZ7.L979125Mo 2004
  [E]—dc22
                                                                    2003011699

10 9 8 7 6 5 4 3 2 1

First published in the United States of America in 2004 by The Kane Press.
Printed in Hong Kong.

Science Solves It! is a registered trademark of The Kane Press.

www.kanepress.com

My cousin, Jenna, is a screamer.
Anything can set her off.

The rest of us were watching TV
when we heard a scream like you wouldn't
believe. Jenna dashed out of the bathroom.

Hey, maybe a crocodile had climbed
up the drainpipe?

3

No such luck! It was just a spider stuck in the bathtub.

Jenna's big brother, Jake, started teasing her like he always does. "SPIDER ATTACK!" he yelled. "RUN FOR YOUR LIVES!"

My sister, Kim, joined in. She trapped the
spider in a cup and jiggled it at Jenna. "Stop it!"
I said.

Jenna and I are the same age. We stick up
for each other—the little kids
against the big kids!

We were going to the beach in the morning. So after dinner the four of us went to the basement to get the beach stuff. We took flashlights. It was dark—and creepy.

Jake poked Jenna. "Hey, I bet this place is full of *bugs*!"

"Leave her alone," I said.

Kim took over. "Kyle, you and Jenna get the beach toys," she told us in her bossiest voice. "Jake and I will get the chairs and umbrella."

I shined my light under the Ping Pong table.
It was like Cardboard City. The box of beach
toys was there. So was a lot of other stuff.
We had to crawl to get to the beach box.
There were all kinds of things in it—even
some sand.

HALLOWEEN

UP

"Listen!" Jenna said.

"What? I don't hear anything," I told her. Then I heard it, too—a scratching noise was coming from the other end of the table.

Something *was* there!

BEACH TOYS

I peeked through the boxes. There was a huge
shadow on the wall. It was coming our way!
Jenna screamed. Her scream made *me* scream.

We ran for the stairs!

"What's going on?" Mom and Dad asked.

"There's a Monster Bug in the basement!"
Jenna told them.

"Under the Ping Pong table!" I added.

Mom gave Jake and Kim a funny look. "Did you two see it?" They both shook their heads, but I could see they were trying not to laugh. That's when I knew they had tricked us.

But how?

Later on I went back down with Dad to get the beach toys. I was doing a little detective work, too. I looked under the Ping Pong table. No Monster Bugs. Not even any ordinary bugs.

Then I saw a plastic bug mixed in with some junk on the table. It reminded me of the Monster Bug. But that was *huge*. This bug was little.

"Kyle!" Jenna called. "We're having ice cream. Come on up before it's all gone!"

I raced upstairs. I wasn't going to let Jake and Kim hog the dessert. They eat like elephants.

The next day we went to the beach—with a lot of stuff. Jenna and I went right into the water. We had so much fun.

When we came out, we wrote our names
in the sand. Then we played ball.
"Look how tall we are!" said Jenna.
She was talking about our shadows
on the wet sand.

object   light

shadow

An umbrella makes a
shadow when it is put
between the sun and
the sand.

When the sun is
low in the sky,
shadows are long.

All morning we ran back and forth between the ocean and our beach blanket. We had to keep putting on sunscreen—Mom's orders!

Dad kept moving the umbrella so the shade would stay on our blanket—and on the lemonade!

8 o'clock   10 o'clock   12 o'clock

The umbrella is tilted less and less as the sun moves higher and higher in the sky.

Jenna and I started building a sand castle.

"Make way for us big guys!" yelled Jake. Kim was right behind him. Their big feet knocked over our tallest tower!

"What creeps!" said Jenna.

"Never mind them," I said. "Let's go back in the water."

We were riding the waves when Mom called us in for lunch. "We'd better hurry," I said. "Kim and Jake are already stuffing their faces."

"Hey, what happened to our shadows?" said Jenna.

I looked down. They were still there, but now they were tiny.

That's when it hit me. "Don't say anything now," I told Jenna. "But I think I know how Jake and Kim tricked us with the Monster Bug."

When the sun is high in the sky, shadows are short.

That night Jenna and I sneaked down to the basement. Kim and Jake were busy watching a scary movie about a mutant cockroach. I asked Jenna to hold the plastic bug up near the wall. Then I shined my flashlight on it.

"The thing we saw was *way* bigger," said Jenna. "And it was moving!"

"Okay, come a little closer," I told her.
The bug's shadow looked bigger.

"Closer," I said, "and wiggle it a little."
"Ta-da!" said Jenna. "Monster Bug!"

"We've *got* to scare them back!" Jenna said. She was right. It was payback time. But what could we do? Hide in the closet? Make a headless body? Dress up like ghosts?

"I could be a giant lobster!" said Jenna. She was holding up my old lobster costume.

"You'd be about as scary as Mr. Potato Head," I said. Then I took another look. I noticed the *shape* of the costume. Jenna the Lobster would make a very scary *shadow*!

We got everything ready, and I went upstairs.

"I found the Monster Bug!" I told Kim and Jake.

Kim smirked. "There's no such thing," she said.

"That's what *I* thought," I said. "But then I found this *huge* nest—and there was something inside it."

Kim and Jake looked a little freaked.

"Something *awful!*" I told them. "And it moved!"

"Show us," they said.

THE END!

I led the way downstairs. "It's over there," I said.

Jake and Kim inched slowly toward the back wall.

They tiptoed closer . . . and closer . . . and . . .

MONSTER BUG!

Jake and Kim grabbed each other and shrieked. I never heard such loud screams in my life—even from Jenna.

Jenna jumped out. "JENNA ATTACK!" she said. "RUN FOR YOUR LIVES!"

Jake and Kim gasped. Then they started laughing. "You really got us," said Jake.

"That's one for you guys," Kim said.

Jenna had a huge smile on her face. I probably did, too. The little kids had tricked the big kids—finally!

THINK LIKE A SCIENTIST

Kyle thinks like a scientist—and so can you!

Scientists observe and ask questions. They look for answers. Sometimes they do tests.

Look Back
On page 22, what did Kyle and Jenna see when they shined the flashlight on the plastic bug? On page 23, what did they do? What did they find out?

Try This!
Can you make a Wall Monster? If you have a flashlight, you can!

Ask a friend to stand in front of a wall and pretend to be a monster. Turn off the lights. Shine the flashlight on your friend:
• from the other side of the room
• from the middle of the room
• and up close

What did you learn about shadows?